# IN THIS NIGHT...

# $\mathscr{I}$N $\mathscr{T}$HIS $\mathscr{N}$IGHT...

## IRMGARD LUCHT

Hyperion Books for Children

New York

Day ends, and quiet spreads over the countryside. The setting sun sinks behind the mountains, taking its light so that night can fall. The moon, the sun's calm and gentle brother, slowly rises higher

and higher. Its soft glow lights up the sky and the secret life
of the night.

This is the night that spring begins. The long, dark winter is over
at last, and everything will be made new.

The sun has set. Its last light lingers, growing gradually paler and paler.

Twilight comes.

This is the hour of blackbirds. One lifts his voice in evening song, a second echoes him. The two of them sing in tireless turns, a continuous round of song. They sing of all that's been gone so long: of spring and meadows full of flowers, of green trees and warm rain.

Even the air smells of spring.

Clouds draw the night in nearer, escorting a flock of wild geese.

Night falls but the city does not yet sleep. Lights come on in the houses and along the streets: first here, then there, then everywhere.

Cats need no light. They see in the dark and can always find each other. Spring makes them prowling and restless, eager to be outside.

"Meow! Meow!" calls the tomcat, and the she-cat answers. "How beautiful you are, Tom." Will he be her mate? Time will tell.

The park is empty. How quiet it is! The evening wind blows through trees and across the water, rocking a pair of swans to sleep.
Do swans have dreams? Perhaps they do — about nests and their

newly hatched young. Or perhaps about flying over wide, wide lakes in beautiful, faraway lands. Or perhaps about colors and lights and sounds we humans will never hear.

What the swans know remains their secret.

In the blue stillness of the countryside, a silver river flows. At night everything seems magical, mysterious, and strange.

The wild geese travel on. Night is their friend, protecting them on their long journey.

They are returning from far away. Spring calls and they know to follow, finding their way without road or rail.

The toads have been buried deep in sleep, burrowed away in their hidden places. The winter was long and they seemed barely alive, so still, as though nothing could wake them. But now spring whispers, ever so softly, and something within them stirs.

They set out at once on a tiring trek, a long trip full of danger. All may not survive, but they know only one thing: they must go back to their pond.

The pond is the place where they were born and where they come home to mate. They will lay their eggs where they themselves were hatched, then turn and head back to the forest.

At night the forest is a world all its own, a dark and sheltering dwelling. The moonlit laurel smells unusually sweet, and the night wind rustles the trees. One tree creaks softly, as though rocking in sleep. An owl hoots, far away.

Night is a good time for the mother boar. She and her young feel safe from their enemies, secure in their forest home.

The owl flies soundlessly through the dark. She is a night hunter.
Her eyes are sharp and her hearing is keen; the better to catch
her prey.

In this first night of spring, a mouse loses his life, a tragedy for
him. But the owl's young are hungry and waiting at home for food.

Mysterious things happen in moonlight. Rabbits meet in an empty field.

Will they dance? It looks that way. But this is a fight, not a dance. The bucks chase each other, box and kick, and don't stop till the stronger wins.

The victor will mate with the doe.

It is night still. But a jubilant song suddenly breaks the silence —
first one voice, then two, soon too many to count. Birds greet the
coming day.

A pair of thrushes nest in the hazelnut bush. The female is careful
to keep her eggs warm, waiting patiently for the day they will hatch.

The bush waits, too, just as the trees do. Its buds have grown thick
and ready to burst. Soon everything will be green again.

Night meets day in the early morning. Chill and shadows still hold the land. But already the sky belongs to the light and its game of ever-changing colors. The clouds start to shine as though the light pours from inside them — dawn is very near.

The sheep have slept beneath this sky, curled against one another for warmth. Now the first light slowly wakes them, and they wait for the full break of day.

At last! The wild geese come to roost, having reached their destination. This is the lake that they call home, and it is here in the reeds that they will breed.

Their flight has ended and so has the night, and with it the long, dark winter. The light returns, and the world is made new—full of color, of hope, of life!

Text and illustrations © 1993 by Ravensburger Buchverlag
Otto Maier GmbH, Germany.
All rights reserved.
Printed in Germany.
© 1992 by Ravensburger Buchverlag Otto Maier GmbH. Postfach 1860
Marktstrasse 22–26. Ravensburg 1. D-7980 Germany.
Original German title: In dieser Nacht.
First published in the United States of America by Hyperion Books
for Children, 114 Fifth Avenue, New York, New York 10011.

First Edition
1 3 5 7 9 10 8 6 4 2

Library of Congress Catalog Card Number: 92-54620
ISBN: 1-56282-408-2

Translation by Frank Jacoby-Nelson.
Adaption by Elizabeth Hollow.

The art for this book is prepared in many layers of acrylic paints to
achieve color blends and give depth to the pictures.
This book is set in 20-point ITC Garamond Light Condensed.